The Case of the Sticky Sticks

A Level 1 Early Reader

Copyright © 2010 Disney Enterprises, Inc.
All Rights Reserved. Based on the *Winnie the Pooh* works, by A.A. Milne and E.H. Shepard
Published by Dalmatian Press, LLC, in conjunction with Disney Enterprises, Inc.

Creative Edge, LLC, 2010. All rights reserved. Printed in the U.S.A.

10 11 12   NGS 10 9 8 7 6 5 4 3 2 1
CE12418

One day, Pooh ate honey.

He ate a lot of honey.

"Now I will play," said Pooh.

"One stick!
Two sticks!
Three sticks!
Pooh Sticks!
I want to play Pooh Sticks!"

A stick for Piglet.

A stick for Roo.

A stick for Eeyore.

A stick for Pooh.

"We will drop the sticks
down, down, down to the brook,"
said Piglet. "Then we will
see them go, go, go!"
"Yay!" said Roo.

"One, two, three—drop sticks!"
called Piglet.
The sticks did not drop.
"Uh-oh," said Eeyore.

"One, two, three—drop sticks!"
called Pooh.
The sticks did not drop.
"Oh, no," said Roo.

"We are stuck to the sticks," said Pooh.
"I will get help," said Piglet.
"I will get the Super Sleuths."

Piglet ran off.

"I am a Super Sleuth,"
said Pooh, "but I am stuck."

Piglet called the Super Sleuths,
Darby, Tigger, and Buster.

SSuuuUUppppperrrr sslllEEEUUtthhs!

"Time to slap my cap!"
said Darby.

"Look at the flag," said Tigger.
"It has Pooh Sticks Bridge."
"Come on!" said Darby. "Let's go!"

"Any time, any place,
The Super Sleuths are on the case!"

"Look!" said Piglet.
"Why are we stuck
to the sticks?"

"Hmmmm…." said Tigger.
"I will look. Aha! I see goo!"
"Goo?" said Roo.
"Yes!" said Tigger.
"The Pooh Sticks
   are goo sticks."

"Pooh, did you get the sticks?"said Darby.

"Yes," said Pooh.

"Did you play in goo, too?" said Darby.

"No," said Pooh. "No goo."

"Think, think, think,"
said Darby.
"What did you do?"

"I did eat," said Pooh.

"Did you eat honey?" said Darby.

"A bit," said Pooh. "Well, a lot."

Darby hugged Pooh.

"Silly ol' bear," she said.

"Did you wash your hands?"

"No," said Pooh.

"Aha!" said Tigger.
"Honey goo is on
Pooh's hands and
on the sticky sticks!
If you wash the sticks,
then all the goo
will come off!"

Wash, wash, wash at the brook.

No sticky hands.

No sticky sticks.

"Now we will all play
Pooh Sticks," said Darby.

"One,
two,
three…
drop sticks!"
called Pooh.

And the sticks
dropped!

Down,

down,

down.

"Yay!" said Roo.

"Woo-hoo!"
said Tigger.

"We Super Sleuths stick
together!" said Darby.
"Oh, thank you," said Pooh.